Jeremy and the Fantastic Flying Machine

Becky Citra
illustrated by Jessica Milne

ORCA BOOK PUBLISHERS

To my husband Larry, for all his support.
B.C.

With love, to G.G., my Grandma.
J.M.

Text copyright © 2008 Becky Citra
Illustrations copyright © 2008 Jessica Milne

Library and Archives Canada Cataloguing in Publication

Citra, Becky
Jeremy and the fantastic flying machine / written by Becky Citra;
illustrated by Jessica Milne.

(Orca echoes)
ISBN 978-1-55143-950-1
I. Milne, Jessica, 1974- II. Title. III. Series.

PS8555.I87J4725 2008   jC813'.54   C2007-907393-X

First published in the United States, 2008
Library of Congress Control Number: 2007942400

Summary: In this fourth book of the Jeremy and the Enchanted Theater series, Jeremy and his cat Aristotle must find their way out of an underground maze and solve the last riddle.

Orca Book Publishers gratefully acknowledges the support for its publishing programs provided by the following agencies: the Government of Canada through the Book Publishing Industry Development Program and the Canada Council for the Arts, and the Province of British Columbia through the BC Arts Council and the Book Publishing Tax Credit.

Typesetting by Teresa Bubela
Cover artwork and interior illustrations by Jessica Milne

ORCA BOOK PUBLISHERS
PO Box 5626, STN. B
VICTORIA, BC CANADA
V8R 6S4

ORCA BOOK PUBLISHERS
PO Box 468
CUSTER, WA USA
98240-0468

www.orcabook.com
Printed and bound in Canada.
11 10 09 08 • 4 3 2 1

The Adventure continues...

A long time ago, people came from everywhere to see the plays at the Enchanted Theater. But when Mr. Magnus bought the theater, things started to go wrong. Mr. Magnus mixed up the plays and changed the endings. Zeus, the king of the Greek gods, was so angry he hurled lightning bolts at the theater. Soon no one came to see the plays.

Today the Enchanted Theater is dusty and silent. But not forgotten. Mr. Magnus and his two friends, Jeremy and the talking cat Aristotle, are working hard to save the theater. In their first time-travel adventure,

Jeremy and Aristotle traveled to Mount Olympus to meet Zeus. Zeus gave them three riddles. He promised that he would stop punishing the theater when all three riddles were solved.

Jeremy and Aristotle traveled into the land of the dead to solve the first riddle. The second riddle took them on a sea voyage on the famous Greek ship, the Argo.

Where will the Enchanted Theater send Jeremy and Aristotle to solve the third riddle?

Chapter One
The Last Riddle

The sun was setting when Jeremy ran to the Enchanted Theater.

Perfect for time travel!

Jeremy hurried past the rows of empty seats. He scrambled onto the stage and sped down the long dark hallway to the little room at the end.

Mr. Magnus was sitting on his stool by the window, surrounded by towers of books. He was holding a scroll made of old parchment.

When Jeremy burst through the door, Mr. Magnus jumped up. "Now we can get started!" he cried.

"Meow," said Aristotle from the top of the blue and gold trunk.

3

Mr. Magnus unrolled the scroll.

"The last riddle," said Jeremy.

"And a real doozer!" said Mr. Magnus. His voice shook. "*I'm round like a ball, but I'm not a toy. Beware, Inventor, and your little boy!*"

"An inventor!" said Jeremy.

"I've read all the books," sighed Mr. Magnus. "I found only one inventor. His name was Daedalus. He lived on a Greek island called Crete."

Jeremy looked at the rows of bright costumes. He looked at the shiny swords and glittering shields.

Which prop would they use to go back in time?

"I've never tried to put on a play about Daedalus," said Mr. Magnus. He sounded worried. "Aristotle, show Jeremy what we found."

Aristotle jumped off the blue and gold trunk.

For the first time, Jeremy noticed old-fashioned letters engraved on the top of the trunk. "*Daedalus and the Fantastic Flying Machine,*" he read out loud.

Mr. Magnus lifted up the lid. "It's empty," he said glumly.

Jeremy's heart sank. Then it gave a little jump. In a shadowy corner at the bottom of the trunk, he spied something. He picked it up. It was a huge golden feather.

The feather felt warm.

Jeremy's fingers tingled.

"Here I go!" he said.

Mr. Magnus stared at Jeremy. "Not yet! I haven't told you about the maze and the mons—"

"I need the backpack!" said Jeremy.

"Oh, dear!" Mr. Magnus picked up a backpack. He slid it over Jeremy's arms.

Aristotle leaped onto Jeremy's shoulders.

"Good-bye! Good-bye!" said Mr. Magnus. "Good luck!"

"Good-bye," said Jeremy.

The room swirled around him.

From far away, he heard Mr. Magnus say, "Watch out for the maze and the mons—"

Everything went black.

Chapter Two
The Road to Knossos

Jeremy blinked.

He and Aristotle were standing on a hill beside a dusty road.

Rows of green vines covered the slopes of the hill. Over the tops of the vines, Jeremy glimpsed brown jagged mountains and the blue sea.

Bunches of purple grapes hung on the vines. Jeremy stuck a grape in his mouth.

"This must be the island of Crete," he said. "Whew, it's hot!"

Aristotle pounced in a high arc. The green tail of a skinny lizard slid under a rock.

"Forget the lizard," said Jeremy. "We've got work to do."

He opened the backpack and peered inside.

"Ball of wool, bottle of Sooper Dooper glue, two pairs of sunglasses," he reported. "Doesn't sound like Mr. Magnus is expecting too much trouble this time."

He pulled out a brown tunic and a pair of sandals. He slid the tunic over his head, took off his runners and strapped on the sandals.

He studied the road. It went three different ways. "We could go left," he said, "to the sea."

"Or right," said Aristotle, "to the mountains."

"Or straight ahead," sighed Jeremy.

They heard the babble of excited voices.

"Hide!" said Aristotle.

Jeremy and Aristotle leaped off the road. They ducked into the grape vines.

A parade of men, women and children came over the hill. Some walked and some rode donkeys. They were loaded down with bundles and bags. One woman carried two brown hens in a basket. At the end of the line trudged a little boy with a goat.

The hens clucked.

The donkeys brayed.

The goat bleated.

The boys and girls shouted.

Where was everybody going? Jeremy crept closer to the road and listened.

"They say the king is furious," said the woman with the hens.

"It's the crazy man's last chance," shouted another. "If he doesn't do it today, there's going to be trouble!"

"Are we almost there?" said a little girl.

"We'll be at Knossos at noon!" announced a man riding a donkey.

Everybody cheered.

The boy at the end of the line poked the goat with a stick. "Hurry up!" he shouted.

Jeremy kept still until the boy and the goat disappeared over the hill.

He jumped up. "Come on!"

Then he froze.

Someone was singing, loudly and out of key. He and Aristotle dived back into the grape vines.

Around the corner bounced a wooden cart pulled by an ox. A tall thin man and a short round man rode on top.

The ox shuffled to a stop. The men stopped singing. They stared at the fork in the road and scratched their heads.

"All roads lead to Knossos," said the tall thin man with a sigh.

"That way is longer." The short man pointed to the road that led to the sea.

"But that way is hotter." The tall man pointed to the road that led to the mountains.

Jeremy stood up. He brushed green leaves from his hair. He pointed straight ahead. "Everybody else went that way."

He stepped out of the vines. "I'm Jeremy." Aristotle landed with a thump on his shoulder. "And this is Aristotle."

"I'm Demos," said the tall man.

"And I'm Yannis," said the short man.

"We're going to the palace at Knossos," said Demos, "to see the crazy man."

A crazy man sounded scary. But they couldn't stay here. Jeremy made up his mind quickly. "So are we!" he said.

"Hop aboard!" said Demos.

Jeremy grabbed his backpack. He and Aristotle scrambled into the cart. They settled themselves on a pile of sacks.

Bump, bump, bump went the ox-cart wheels.

Jeremy leaned against a sack. He thought about the riddle. *I'm round like a ball, but I'm not a toy. Beware, Inventor, and your little boy!*

Someone at Knossos had to know the answer!

Bump, bump, bump.

After a long time, they came to the end of the road. They climbed out of the cart.

12

"Wow!" cried Jeremy. Before them was a huge palace with great red pillars. A crowd had gathered outside the palace walls.

Everyone was staring up.

Jeremy looked up too.

A little man stood above them on a balcony. A giant blue kite was strapped to his back.

"There he is!" said Demos. "The crazy man!"

At the front of the crowd, a man in a long robe raised one hand high in the air.

"That's the King of Knossos," whispered Yannis.

The crazy man took a step forward.

A hush fell over the crowd.

"He's going to jump!" shouted Jeremy.

Chapter Three
The Crazy Man

The man on the balcony took a step back.

The crowd groaned.

"He's losing his nerve," said Yannis.

"He's tried four times already," said Demos. "All disasters. That kite doesn't look any better than the last one."

"He told the King of Knossos that he can fly," said Yannis. "The king has bragged all over Greece. He wants to be famous."

"If the crazy man fails," said Demos, "he'll be thrown in the maze."

The maze? thought Jeremy. Where had he heard that before?

"Mazes are fun," he said. "I'm good at doing mazes."

Demos and Yannis stared at him. "A maze might be fun," said Demos, "but what about the mons—"

Just then the crowd went, "OOOHHHHH!"

And then, "AAAAHHHH!"

"There he goes!" shouted Jeremy.

Aristotle put his paws over his eyes. "I can't look!"

The crazy man leaped off the balcony.

WHOOOOSH! The blue kite dived toward the ground.

The crowd gasped.

WHIIIIZZZZZ! A sudden gust of wind caught the kite, and it shot up. The crazy man waved bravely at the people below.

"He's flying!" yelled a boy in the crowd.

The kite twisted and turned.

It flipped and flopped.

Then it drifted to the ground like a falling leaf.

The crazy man landed at the foot of the King of Knossos in a jumble of broken kite sticks and tangled string.

The king's face turned purple. Jeremy held his breath.

Then the king roared, "I'll give you one more chance, Daedalus! ONE MORE CHANCE! Tomorrow at noon. Now back to your tower!"

Jeremy's heart jumped. The crazy man was Daedalus the inventor!

"Wait!" Jeremy shouted. "Don't go. I have to talk to you!"

Jeremy pushed his way through the crowd. Daedalus was gathering up pieces of his smashed kite.

Daedalus stared at Jeremy.

The king stared at Jeremy. His eyes were like ice. "And who are you?" he said.

Jeremy's legs felt like jelly. He wanted to turn and run. But he had to save the Enchanted Theater.

"Err...I'm Jeremy," he stammered. "I traveled back in time three thousand years to get here...and Aristotle who lives in the Enchanted Theater came with me and—"

"Spies!" said the king. "Trying to steal my invention!"

A murmur ran through the crowd.

"No, you've got it wrong," said Jeremy. "There's a riddle—"

"GUARDS!" bellowed the king.

"Run!" yelled Aristotle.

Chapter Four
Inside the Maze

Jeremy raced after Aristotle.

Footsteps pounded.

Swords clanked.

The King of Knossos bellowed, "Don't let them get away!"

"This way!" shouted Jeremy. Then he skidded to a stop. More guards were pouring out of the palace.

Jeremy squeezed between the gaping spectators. He spun around. Where was Aristotle?

He spotted a streak of orange disappearing through an open doorway in the palace wall.

Behind him, the king yelled, "There they are! After the spies!"

Jeremy dashed through the doorway.

CRASH! The huge wooden door slammed shut.

CLANK! Iron bolts slid across.

Jeremy's heart pounded. He was standing at the top of a narrow staircase. A strange bluish light glowed from the stone walls.

"Pssst!" hissed a voice. "Down here!"

Jeremy peered down the staircase. Aristotle was crouching in the shadows on the third step. His fur was ruffled.

Jeremy looked back at the massive door. It would never budge. And besides, on the other side were the guards and the king.

He took a big breath. "These stairs have to go somewhere," he said.

Down, down, down into the shadows crept Jeremy and Aristotle. The blue light lit their way.

The stairs ended in a narrow tunnel.

"We must be way under the palace by now," said Jeremy.

Just ahead of them, the tunnel branched in four different directions.

"We'll go left," said Jeremy.

But they had walked only a few steps when the tunnel branched again. This time it went in five directions.

"This must be the maze," said Jeremy. "I'm good at mazes."

Aristotle flicked his tail. "Mr. Magnus said something about the maze and the mons...I forget the rest."

"That's what Demos said too." Jeremy shrugged. "It probably wasn't important."

He peered up one of the tunnels. It looked creepy. But he knew what he had to do. He dug in the backpack and took out the ball of wool.

"Hold onto the end of the wool," he told Aristotle. "If anyone opens the door, yank on the wool. I'll keep walking and look for another way out."

Jeremy set off, unrolling the ball of wool as he walked. His eyes were getting used to the blue light. Every few minutes, the tunnel veered off in different directions.

The maze was an eerie place. A rat scurried past Jeremy's feet. Somewhere in the shadows water dripped. It was hard to keep going.

Jeremy was almost glad when he came to the end of the wool. He started back, rolling it up as he went.

Suddenly, the wool gave a jerk. It danced up and down.

"Aristotle!" His heart racing, Jeremy ran around a bend.

The wool lay in tangles around the cat. Aristotle batted a piece with his paw.

"You were supposed to wait at the door!" said Jeremy. "And why have you tangled everything up?"

"Because that's what cats do with wool," said Aristotle coldly. He flicked a strand of wool off his ear. "You were ages."

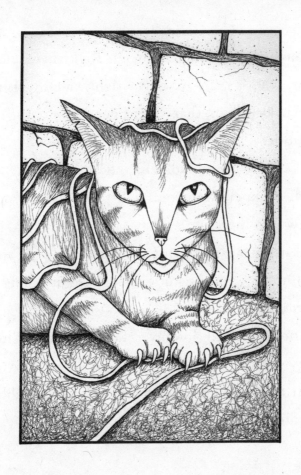

"We're going back," said Jeremy. "We'll knock on the door until the king lets us out."

Jeremy freed Aristotle from the tangle of wool. He chanted out loud as they made their way back through the winding tunnels. "Right here…left… right…this is the way…left…right…almost there."

"Lucky for us that you're good at mazes," said Aristotle.

"Left! No, right! No, left!" said Jeremy.

He stopped. Someone had scratched a crooked arrow into the stone wall.

"I never saw that before," he said.

"Or this," said Aristotle. He picked up a long thin object. "It looks like a—"

"Bone!" cried Jeremy. "Look! Bones! They're everywhere!"

At that moment, they heard a thundering blood-curdling roar.

Chapter Five
The Monster

Jeremy and Aristotle froze.

"We've got to get out of here," hissed Aristotle.

"Follow the arrow," said Jeremy shakily. "Go left!"

Jeremy and Aristotle crept along the tunnel. After a few minutes, they spotted a second arrow scratched into the stone.

"Left again," said Jeremy.

And then, a moment later, "Left!"

Jeremy stopped trembling. "I think we're getting somewhere," he said.

He peered ahead. "Another arrow! Left again!"

Jeremy started to run.

"Another left!" he shouted.

And then he skidded to a stop. He looked around.

Bones everywhere!

A crooked arrow!

"We're back where we started!" cried Jeremy.

"So much for being good at mazes," said Aristotle.

RRRRRAAAAARRRRRGGGGGHHHHHH!

Jeremy and Aristotle jumped. "Go right," said Jeremy, "and don't make any noise."

Jeremy and Aristotle tiptoed along the tunnel. "Turn right again," whispered Jeremy. "And right here." He shivered as he kicked a pile of bones. "Another right."

Jeremy peered ahead. "I think we're coming to a room—"

RRRRRRRRAAAAAAAARRRRRGGGGHHH!

A huge shape lunged out of the shadows.

Long pointed horns flashed in the blue light.

Red eyes glowed like embers.

The thing snorted and growled. It blew steam from its wide nostrils.

"A MONSTER!" yelled Jeremy and Aristotle.

They spun around and ran.

Heavy footsteps thumped after them. The tunnel echoed with the monster's snarls.

They came to another fork in the maze of tunnels. Aristotle veered to the right. "Hurry!" he shouted.

Jeremy's sandal kicked at some more bones.

He stopped, his heart pounding. He picked up two bones.

It was their only chance.

He counted in his head. One…two…three…

He flung the bones up the left tunnel. They hit the stone wall with a loud rattle just as the monster thundered around the corner.

With a roar, it chased after the bones.

Jeremy sped up the right tunnel. He caught up to Aristotle. "I tricked the monster," he said, "but we better—"

Jeremy's heart lurched.

Aristotle was crouching in front of a brick wall.

A dead end!

Chapter Six
The Secret Door

RRRRRAAAAARRRRGGGHHHHH!

The hair stood up on Aristotle's back. "I don't think the monster liked your trick," he said.

Jeremy kept his eyes on the tunnel. He backed against the brick wall.

There was a loud grating sound. Jeremy felt the wall move. He tumbled through a space that opened up between the bricks. He landed with a bump at the bottom of a winding staircase.

Aristotle leaped after him.

"It's a secret door!" said Jeremy. Before he could blink, the bricks slid together.

A muffled roar on the other side of the wall faded away.

Jeremy looked up. The winding stairs disappeared into the blue shadows.

Aristotle flicked his tail. "I'll stay here while you—"

"You're coming with me!" said Jeremy. "You got us into this mess."

Up and up, around and around climbed Jeremy and Aristotle.

The stairs ended at a small wooden door.

Jeremy put his ear against the door. He heard a rattling sound, like marbles rolling together.

"Whoever is in there sounds busy," said Aristotle. "Let's come back some other—"

Jeremy grabbed Aristotle's tail. He knocked on the door.

He waited a few seconds. Then he pushed it open. He peered into a small round room.

In one corner were two bulky objects covered in cloth. In another corner lay the broken kite.

A man stood at the window with his back to them. A small boy was kneeling on the floor in front of a contraption made of chutes and tunnels and slides.

Flap, flap, flap. A blue bird flew away from the windowsill.

"Bye-bye, birdie," said the boy.

The man watched the bird fly away. He scratched some numbers on a clay tablet.

The little boy picked up a round pebble and dropped it down a chute. It rattled and slid all the way to the floor.

He clapped his hands. Then he looked up. "Nice kitty!" he said.

Aristotle's fur ruffled. The man at the window turned around.

It was the crazy man!

His eyes brightened. "The time travelers," he said. "You found your way to my secret door! I'm Daedalus, and this is my son Icarus. Welcome to our tower."

Chapter Seven
Daedalus and Icarus

"I must finish my notes," said Daedalus. "Then we can talk."

Jeremy looked around while he waited. The room was brimming with wonderful things.

Wheels and cogs.

Gears and springs.

Candles and burners and pieces of pipe.

Models of dragonflies, butterflies and bumblebees cluttered the shelves. A skeleton of a raven rested on a table. A huge stuffed eagle gazed down from a wooden perch.

Jeremy kneeled beside Icarus. "I have a game just like this at home," he said.

Daedalus wrote busily on his tablet. A swallow landed on the windowsill and preened itself. It dropped a brown feather.

"Swallows! Wonderful aerodynamics!" said the inventor. He scooped up the feather.

He put his writing materials and the feather on a table. "I have a few ideas of my own about time travel. You must tell me how you got here."

Jeremy told Daedalus the story of Mr. Magnus and the Enchanted Theater and Zeus's punishment.

Daedalus's eyes shone. "A magical theater! I can imagine it perfectly. But what a pity you don't know the exact method for time travel."

Jeremy shrugged. "It just happens. I hold on to one of the actor's props and everything spins around."

"Must have something to do with the speed of light and the density of the atmosphere," said Daedalus. "I have a theory that I could test."

"I haven't told you everything," said Jeremy. "The last riddle. You and Icarus are in it!"

He said slowly, "*I'm round like a ball, but I'm not a toy. Beware, Inventor, and your little boy!*"

Daedalus blinked. "A warning from Zeus! I bet the King of Knossos is behind this."

"What do you think it means?" said Jeremy.

"I don't know, but I don't trust the king one bit!" said Daedalus.

"Me neither," said Jeremy. Aristotle twitched his tail.

"I designed the maze for the king," said Daedalus. "I planned the whole thing, right down to the blue lights." He chuckled. "The lights are one of my better inventions. It's because of the mineral in the rock and…now, where was I?"

"You designed the maze," said Jeremy helpfully.

Daedalus frowned. "I didn't know it was for the Minotaur!"

"You mean the monster!" said Jeremy. "It almost caught us."

"The Minotaur is half-bull and half-man," said Daedalus. "It lives in the middle of the maze. The king sacrifices fourteen men every year. He throws them into the maze, and they're never seen again."

Jeremy remembered the bones. He shivered right down to his toes.

"I suspected the king was up to no good," said Daedalus. "That's why I put in the secret door. I was afraid that Icarus and I might be thrown in the maze too."

"Why don't you leave?" asked Jeremy.

"The king has guards at all the harbors," said Daedalus. "He's keeping me a prisoner so I won't tell anyone how to get out of the maze."

"And now you're in danger," said Jeremy. He couldn't stop thinking about the riddle.

"There is only one way that Icarus and I can escape from the Island of Crete," said Daedalus.

He leaned closer to Jeremy. "We can fly!"

Chapter Eight
The Fantastic Flying Machine

Jeremy looked at the ruined kite in the corner of the room. "I'm sorry about your kite," he said. "It almost worked."

Daedalus chuckled. "That thing! It never stood a chance. I made sure that the tail was wrong."

"You did that on purpose?" asked Jeremy.

"I needed more time," said Daedalus. "You see, the king thinks I'm working on the kite."

"So what *are* you doing up here?" asked Jeremy.

Daedalus walked over to the cloth-covered objects in the corner of the room. "Do you want to see a real flying machine?"

Jeremy's eyes glowed. "Sure!"

Daedalus swept the cloth off the biggest object. Underneath was a huge pair of wings. They were made out of feathers that were all the colours of the rainbow. A leather harness with levers was strapped underneath the wings.

Jeremy touched one of the wings. "It's fantastic!"

"A fantastic flying machine!" said Daedalus. "That's what it is indeed!"

Icarus clapped his hands. "Me too!"

Daedalus beamed. He uncovered the second object. It was a pair of wings the same as the first pair but much smaller.

"I've been giving Icarus lessons on how to work the controls," said Daedalus. "Watch."

He pulled one of the levers.

"Up!" said Icarus.

He pulled another lever.

"Down!" said Icarus.

Daedalus patted Icarus's head. "That's my boy! I've also built in controls for wind speed and changes in weather."

"It's the best invention ever!" said Jeremy.

"I am a little ahead of my time," said Daedalus. "And now...according to my flight plan, we leave at sunrise tomorrow. That gives us...let's see...just enough time. Of course, you'll have to share. There's no way we can make two pairs of wings."

Jeremy's heart jumped. "You mean—"

"You and Aristotle are coming with us," said Daedalus. "Did you really think I would leave you behind?"

"Wow!" said Jeremy.

Aristotle purred.

"There's no time to lose," said Daedalus.

He bustled around the room. He put pieces of leather, scraps of wood and a sack full of feathers on a long workbench.

"Stick your arms out, my boy," said Daedalus, "so I can see the size."

Jeremy put both arms out. He turned around slowly while Daedalus jotted numbers on a clay tablet.

"Are there enough feathers?" said Jeremy, worried.

"More than enough! Every bird in Knossos has visited my tower. I give them sunflower seeds for a feather or two. It's a fair trade!"

Daedalus worked on the wooden frame for the wings. Jeremy sorted the feathers into piles that were small, medium and big.

He listened carefully while Daedalus explained about airflow and updraft and downdraft.

At supper time, Daedalus set out bread, honey and cups of milk. He lit a lantern when the sky turned dark. Icarus fell asleep in a small cot, and Aristotle curled up beside him.

Daedalus and Jeremy worked on. Daedalus stitched the harness. Jeremy arranged the feathers in neat rows on the frame.

"I've been using melted wax to stick the feathers together," said Daedalus. "I hope we have enough time for it to set."

Jeremy ran to his backpack. He took out the bottle of Sooper Dooper Glue. He read the words on the

side of the bottle. "Sets instantly. Perfect for wood, cloth, paper and plastic. It doesn't say anything about feathers, but I'm sure it will work."

"Paper? Plastic?" said Daedalus. "You must tell me about those sometime."

While they glued feathers, Daedalus tested Jeremy.

"How do you stop from rolling?"

"Keep the wings level."

"What makes you stall?"

"Not enough wing beats per minute."

"What do you remember about takeoff?"

"Face into the wind."

At last the wings were finished. Jeremy tried them on. They quivered as if they were alive.

Daedalus looked longingly at the bottle of Sooper Dooper Glue. "I must try to invent some of that."

"You can keep it!" said Jeremy.

His eyes gleaming, Daedalus popped the bottle into a pocket in his tunic.

"Now, dear boy, you need some sleep. I'll stay up and keep watch."

Jeremy nestled in with Icarus and Aristotle. Daedalus settled into his chair, yawning.

"I'm not tired," said Jeremy. He kept opening his eyes to peek at his wings.

The next thing he knew, someone was shaking his shoulder. Sunlight streamed through the window.

"We've all slept in!" said Daedalus. "It's past noon! We've got to leave! Now!"

Chapter Nine
Beware, Inventor

Daedalus climbed up a ladder. He opened a trapdoor in the ceiling.

He carried Icarus up the ladder and through the trapdoor. Jeremy slipped on his backpack. He and Aristotle scrambled after them onto the roof of the tower.

Then Daedalus went back for the wings. He passed them through the trapdoor to Jeremy.

Daedalus strapped the small pair of wings on Icarus. He helped Jeremy with his wings. Aristotle leaped on top of Jeremy's backpack.

Then Daedalus put on his wings. He clipped one end of a rope to Icarus's belt and the other end to his own belt.

They were ready.

The sun was high in the sky. A brisk wind blew. A crowd had gathered outside the palace. The King of Knossos paced back and forth.

Suddenly a boy shouted, "The crazy man! He's on top of that tower!"

"The crazy man! The crazy man!" the people cried.

The king glared up at the tower. "DAEDALUS!" he bellowed. "YOU'RE LATE! AND HOW DID YOU GET UP THERE?"

"This is it, Jeremy," said Daedalus. "Off you go! We'll be right behind you."

Jeremy looked down. He felt dizzy. His tummy did a flip-flop.

"I can't," he whispered.

Then he remembered something. In the Enchanted Theater Rule Book it said that only a hero can time travel.

Jeremy was a hero, and heroes can do anything they want.

He faced into the wind.

He took a big breath.

He sprang off the tower roof.

For a second, Jeremy forgot everything Daedalus had told him. He forgot to count the wing beats. He forgot about updraft and downdraft. He forgot to keep the wings level.

ZOOOOOOOMMMM!

His flying machine streaked toward the gaping crowd. Aristotle closed his eyes. He dug his claws into the backpack. People ducked and ran for cover.

Jeremy pulled one of the levers.

WHOOOOSH!

Up they soared!

Higher and higher.

Far below, the crowd cheered.

"I think I've got the hang of it," said Jeremy.

He looked back. Daedalus and Icarus flew side by side, held together with the rope. Daedalus gave Jeremy a thumbs-up.

"Now for a loop-de-loop," said Jeremy. "Hang on, Aristotle!"

He moved the controls like an expert.

WHOOSH...ZOOOOM...WHIIIZZZZ!

The flying machine whirled in circles. It dipped up and down and back and forth.

Jeremy made a huge figure eight over the king's head.

The king waved his fist. "WHAT ARE YOU DOING?" he hollered.

"I'M FLYING!" Jeremy yelled back.

He made one more turn and then soared off into the blue sky. He and Aristotle led the way. Daedalus and Icarus followed close behind.

They left the palace of Knossos. They flew over the green fields and over the brown mountains, all the way to the sea.

The sun blazed down on the sparkling blue water. The wind blew in Jeremy's face. He felt as powerful as an eagle.

"Flying is the life for me!" he cried.

"No more loop-de-loops," said Aristotle. "I want to go home!"

"It says in the Enchanted Rule Book that a hero must do five brave things to return home," Jeremy reminded him.

"You hitched a ride with Yannis and Demos," said Aristotle. "That's one."

"I tried to tell the king about the riddle," said Jeremy. "That's two."

"You tricked the Minotaur, and you jumped off the tower first," said Aristotle. "That takes care of three and four."

Just then, Jeremy heard Daedalus cry out. He turned his wings.

The rope between Daedalus and his son was stretched tight. Icarus jiggled the clip at the end of the rope.

"NO, ICARUS!" Daedalus shouted. "DON'T TOUCH IT!"

But it was too late. Icarus gave the clip a tug. The end of the rope dropped free.

The little boy spun in a circle.

"Help!" he screamed.

Then he shot up.

Up, up, up. Straight toward the blazing sun.

"He's too light!" said Daedalus. "He doesn't have enough ballast."

Daedalus pulled a lever. But his wings didn't move. "My machine's jammed," he said. "The rope's tangled everything up!"

Just then, a red feather drifted down from the sky. And a yellow feather.

"The sun's melting the wax on Icarus's wings!" said Daedalus.

Horrified, Jeremy watched another feather twirl out of the sky.

He had to save Icarus!

"Hang on, Aristotle!" he shouted. "We're going up!"

Chapter Ten
The Fifth Brave Thing

Jeremy tilted his wings toward the sun. He couldn't see Icarus. He couldn't see anything in the blazing light.

"Get the sunglasses, Aristotle!" he said.

Aristotle dug in the backpack.

Two more feathers drifted down.

A tingle ran up Jeremy's spine. What would the sun do to Sooper Dooper Glue?

Jeremy put on a pair of sunglasses. Aristotle put on the other pair.

"Full speed ahead!" said Jeremy.

ZOOOOOM.

Straight into the sun.

Higher and higher they flew.

Jeremy could feel the rays burning his face.

Then something spun out of the sky. It was Icarus. Jeremy caught him like a football.

"Father!" wailed the little boy.

Jeremy made a tight turn. He glided back to Daedalus.

Daedalus had untangled the rope. He took Icarus from Jeremy's arms.

"Thank you, my dear boy. Thank you," said Daedalus.

Jeremy wanted to say, "No problem."

But just then, everything went black.

Jeremy opened his eyes. He was in the little room in the Enchanted Theater. Aristotle washed his fur by the window.

"You're home!" said Mr. Magnus.

"I saved Icarus," said Jeremy. "That was my fifth brave thing. But I didn't solve the riddle."

Mr. Magnus's face fell. "It was the hardest one," he said kindly.

He picked up the scroll. He read out loud, "*I'm round like a ball, but I'm not a toy. Beware, Inventor, and your little boy.*"

"Meow!" said Aristotle. He batted his paw against the window. Outside, the sunset was orange and red.

"That's it!" said Jeremy. "The answer is the sun. The sun melted Icarus's wings!"

Jeremy and Mr. Magnus and Aristotle looked at the lightning bolt in the corner of the room. It glowed with a dazzling light.

"It's the sign from Zeus," said Jeremy. "We got it right!"

Aristotle purred.

Mr. Magnus beamed. "It looks like the Enchanted Theater is back in business!"

Chapter Eleven
Bravo!

The Enchanted Theater was ablaze with lights. Above the big doors, a sign said *Daedalus and the Fantastic Flying Machine. Held over by popular demand.*

Inside the theater, the velvet curtain closed across the great stage.

There was a storm of clapping.

Jeremy clapped the hardest of all. He was sitting in the front row between Mr. Magnus and Aristotle. It was the best play he had ever seen.

"Encore!" someone yelled. "Encore!"

"It's the fifth curtain call," boasted Mr. Magnus. He was dressed in his fine evening suit.

Jeremy waited for the curtain to open one more time. He held his breath.

59

Suddenly something tiny and gray scurried out from under the curtain. A mouse! Aristotle saw it too. He leaped off his seat.

"No, Aristotle," whispered Jeremy.

But it was too late. Aristotle bounded onto the stage.

Someone in the audience laughed. Then more people laughed.

Jeremy slid off his seat. "Come back, Aristotle," he hissed.

He climbed onto the stage. The mouse had disappeared. Aristotle was batting the edge of the curtain.

Jeremy grabbed Aristotle.

At that moment, the curtains fell open. A spotlight shone in Jeremy's face.

On each side of him, the actors and actresses held hands. They raised them over their heads.

The roar of clapping echoed to the high ceiling.

Mr. Magnus stood up. "Three cheers for Jeremy and Aristotle!" he cried.

Everyone stood up. The theater rang with their cries.

"Bravo!"

"Bravo!"

"Hooray for Jeremy and Aristotle!"

Aristotle purred. Jeremy blinked in the bright lights.
Then he did the only thing he could do.

He bowed.

Becky Citra is the author of *Jeremy and the Enchanted Theater*, the first book in the Jeremy series. She is also the author of the Max and Ellie books, Orca Young Readers set in nineteenth-century Upper Canada. She lives in Bridge Lake, British Columbia.